SYLVESTER M
W9-CEW-431

HIGHLINE SCHOOL DISTRICT
3 2175 00920 9992

Wheels, Wings, and Water

# Trains

Lola M. Schaefer

Heinemann Library
Chicago, Illinois

a division of Reed Elsevier Inc.
Chicago, Illinois

Customer Service 888-454-2279
Visit our website at www.heinemannlibrary.com



Designed by Sue Emerson, Heinemann Library; Page layout by Que-Net Media
Printed and bound in the United States by Lake Book Manufacturing, Inc.
Photo research by Amor Montes De Oca

07 06 05 04
10 9 8 7 6 5 4 3 2

**Library of Congress Cataloging-in-Publication Data**
Schaefer, Lola M., 1950-
Trains / Lola M. Schaefer.
v. cm. – (Wheels, wings, and water)
Includes index.
Contents: What are trains? – What do trains look like? – What are trains made of? – How did trains look long ago? – What is a passenger train? – What is a freight train? – What is a subway? – What is a high-speed train? – What are some special trains? – Quiz – Picture glossary.
ISBN 1-4034-0885-8 (HC) , 1-4034-3624-X (Pbk.)
1. Railroads–Juvenile literature. [1. Railroads–Trains.] I. Title. II. Series.
TF148.S38 2003
625.1–dc21
2002014727

**Acknowledgments**
The author and publishers are grateful to the following for permission to reproduce copyright material:
pp. 4, 7L Gary J. Benson; p. 5 Royalty-Free/Corbis; p. 6 Colin Garratt/Milepost 921/2/Corbis; pp. 7R, 15R Dr. Alan K. Mallams; p. 8 Kent Foster/Visuals Unlimited; p. 9 Lee Foster/Bruce Coleman, Inc.; p. 10 Corbis; p. 11 Hulton Archive/Getty Images; p. 12 Matt Bradley/Bruce Coleman, Inc.; pp. 13, 20 Jeff Greenberg/Visuals Unlimited; pp. 14, 22, 24 Reed Saxon/AP Wide World Photos; p. 15L Edmond Van Hoorick/Getty Images; p. 16 Art Stein/Corbis; p. 17 Richard T. Nowitz/Corbis; p. 18 Angela Rowlings/AP Wide World Photo; p. 19 Michael S. Yamashita/Corbis; p. 21 Reuters Photo Archive/NewsCom; p. 23 row 1 (L-R) Reed Saxon/AP Wide World Photo, Reuters Photo Archive/NewsCom, Matt Bradley/Bruce Coleman, Inc., Gary J. Benson; row 2 (L-R) Dr. Alan K. Mallams, PhotoDisc, Corbis, D. Long/Visuals Unlimited; row 3 (L-R) Dr. Alan K. Mallams, Jeff Greenberg/Visuals Unlimited, Colin Garratt/Milepost 921/2/Corbis, Jeff Greenberg/Visuals Unlimited; row 4 (L-R) Corbis, Hulton Archive/Getty Images; back cover (L-R) D. Long/Visuals Unlimited, Gary J. Benson

Cover photograph by Colin Garratt/Milepost 921/2/Corbis

Every effort has been made to contact copyright holders of any material reproduced in this book. Any omissions will be rectified in subsequent printings if notice is given to the publisher.

Special thanks to our advisory panel for their help in the preparation of this book:

Alice Bethke, Library Consultant
Palo Alto, CA

Eileen Day, Preschool Teacher
Chicago, IL

Kathleen Gilbert,
Second Grade Teacher
Round Rock, TX

Sandra Gilbert,
Library Media Specialist
Fiest Elementary School
Houston, TX

Jan Gobeille,
Kindergarten Teacher
Garfield Elementary
Oakland, CA

Angela Leeper,
Educational Consultant
North Carolina Department
of Public Instruction
Wake Forest, NC

Some words are shown in bold, **like this.**
You can find them in the picture glossary on page 23.

# Contents



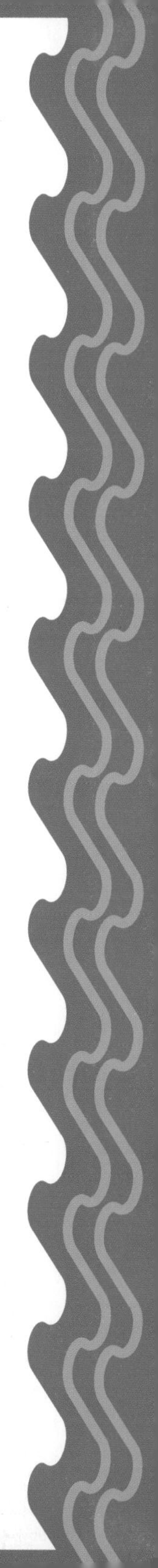

# What Are Trains?

Trains are **railroad cars** hooked together.

They can carry people or things.

Each railroad car has wheels that roll on a **track.**

**Locomotives** push or pull trains.

# What Do Trains Look Like?

Trains look like long lines of **rectangles.**

**Railroad cars** on trains can be short or tall.

**Tank cars** look like long tubes.

**Flatcars** have no sides or top.

# What Are Trains Made Of?

Most trains are made of metal.

Some trains are made of wood.

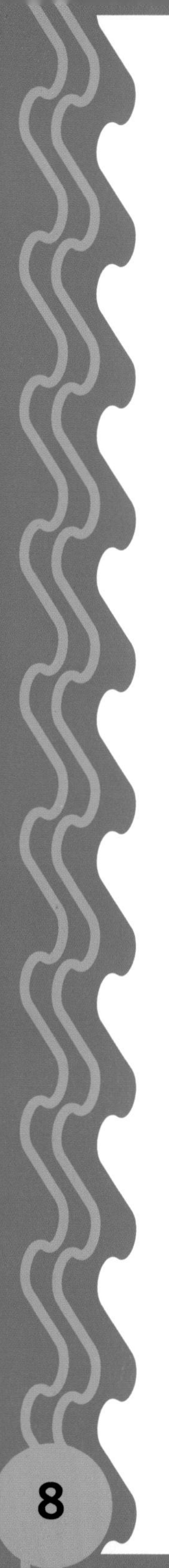

The wheels of a train are made of metal.

Train **tracks** are metal, too.

# How Did Trains Look Long Ago?

The first trains looked like wagons.

People could sit outside the cars.

Later, **steam engines** pulled cars shaped like boxes.

People rode inside these trains.

# What Is a Passenger Train?

A **passenger** train carries many people.

The **railroad cars** on passenger trains are called coaches.

People can eat in the dining coach.

They can sleep in the sleeping coach.

# What Is a Freight Train?

A freight train carries things or animals.

Freight trains pull different kinds of **railroad cars.**

**Boxcars** carry things in cars that look like boxes.

**Hopper cars** can carry coal or corn.

# What Is a Subway?

A subway is an underground train.

Subways move through **tunnels** under big cities.

Many people ride subways to work.

Subways are faster than cars.

# What Is a High-Speed Train?

A high-speed train goes very fast.

It can take people far away in a short time.

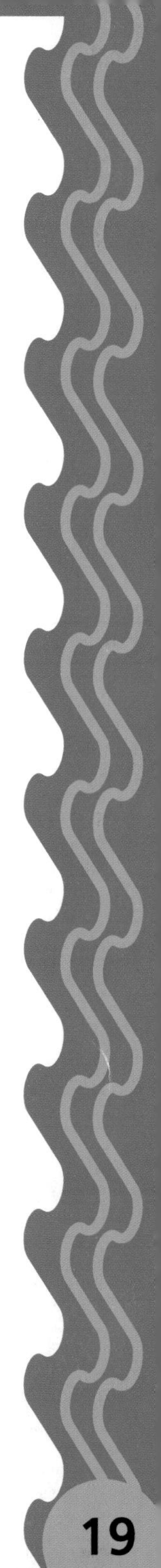

Some high-speed trains have different shapes.

This train looks like a long, smooth **oval**.

# What Are Some Special Trains?

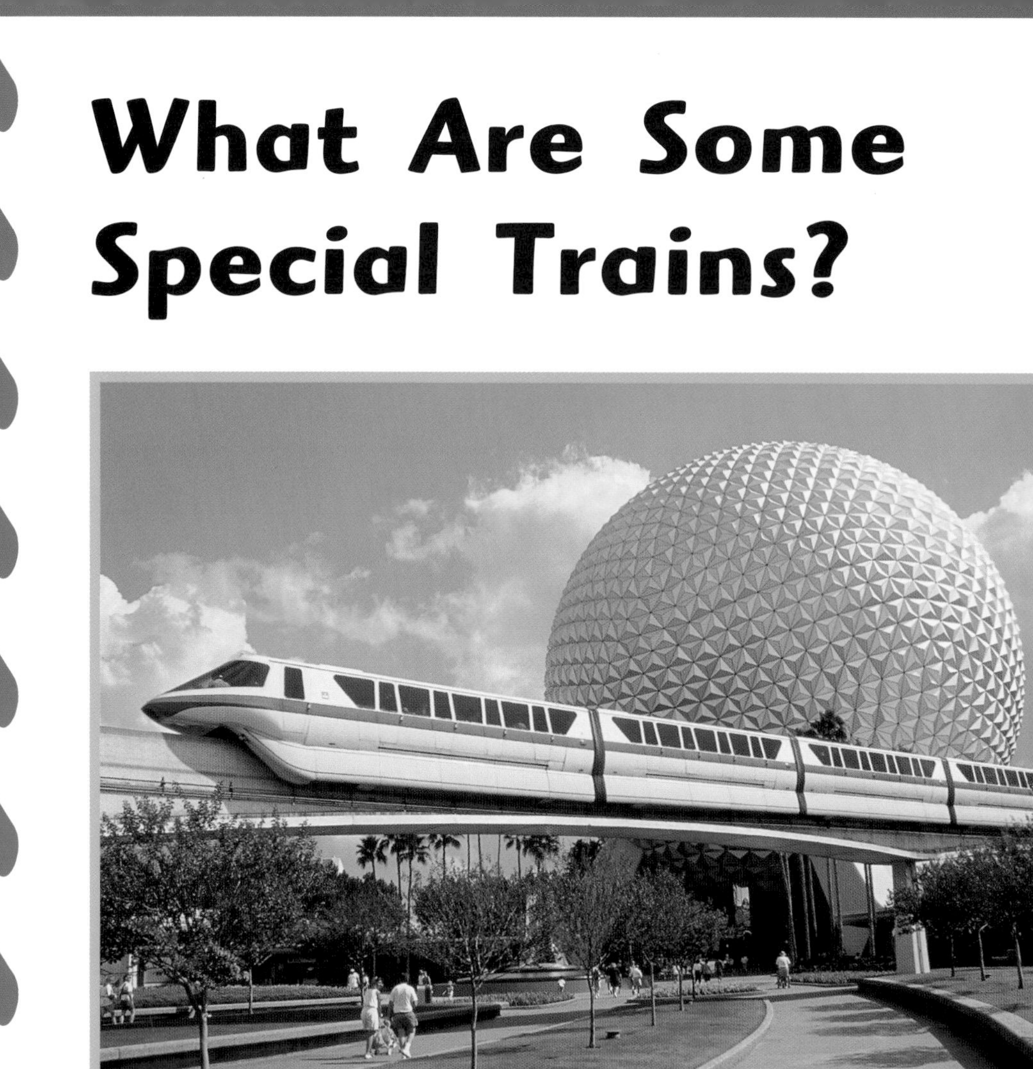

**Monorails** are trains that run on one **track.**

They carry people high above the ground.

**Maglev trains** float on air above a metal **track.**

**Magnets** pull the trains forward.

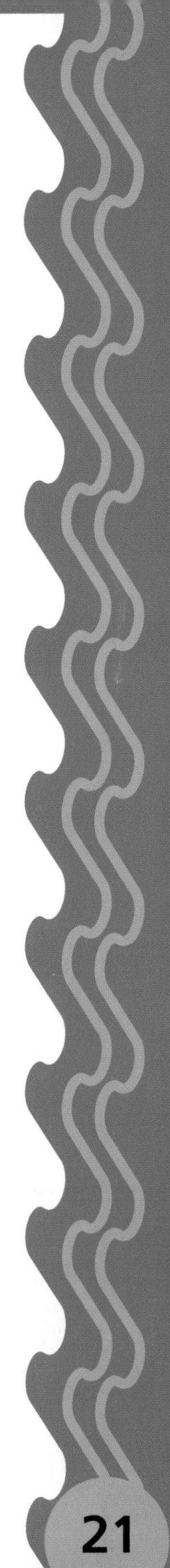

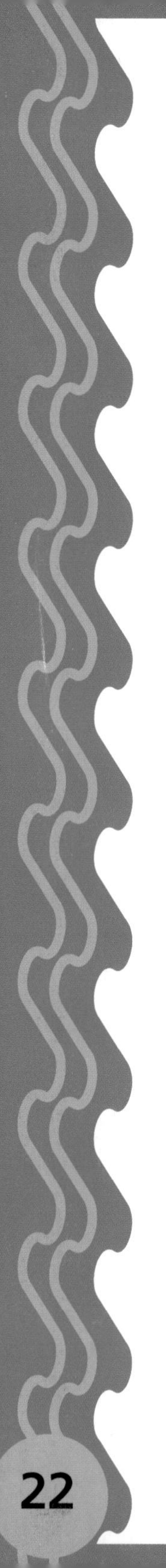

# Quiz

Do you know what kind of train this is?

Can you find it in the book?

Look for the answer on page 24.

# Picture Glossary

**boxcar**
page 15

**maglev train**
page 21

**passengers**
page 12

**tank car**
page 7

**flatcar**
page 7

**magnet**
page 21

**railroad car**
pages 4, 6, 12, 14

**track**
pages 5, 9, 20–21

**hopper car**
page 15

**monorail**
page 20

**rectangle**
page 6

**tunnel**
page 16

**locomotive**
page 5

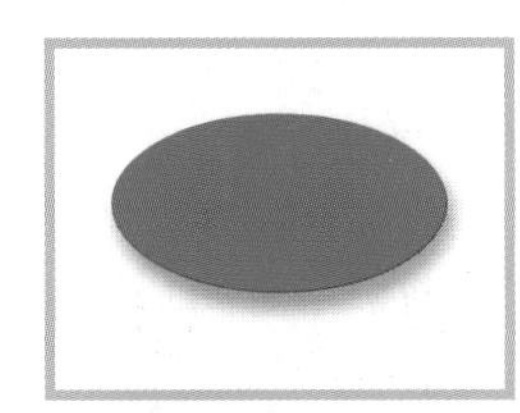

**oval**
page 19

**steam engine**
page 11

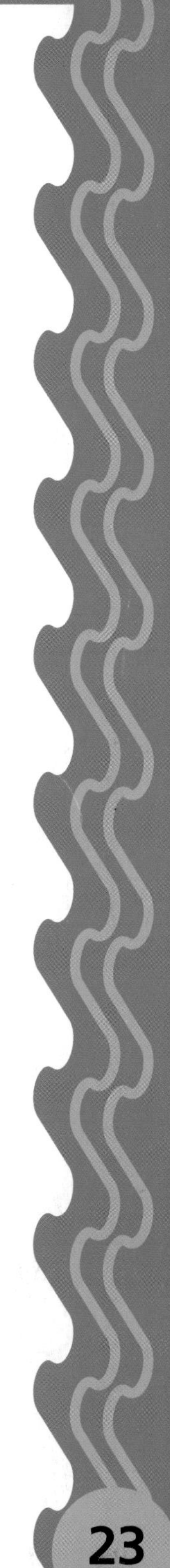

# Note to Parents and Teachers

Reading for information is an important part of a child's literacy development. Learning begins with a question about something. Help children think of themselves as investigators and researchers by encouraging their questions about the world around them. Each chapter in this book begins with a question. Read the question together. Talk about what you think the answer might be. Read the text to find out if your predictions were correct. Think of other questions you could ask about the topic, and discuss where you might find the answers. In this book, the picture glossary symbol for vehicle is a train. Explain to children that a vehicle is something that can move people or things from one place to another. Some vehicles have motors, like cars, but others do not.

# Index



**Answer to quiz on page 22**

This is a freight train.